To: Seven

Thanks for your work with L.A.C.E.S. & the Kick Out Corruption campaign. In solidarity, Robtel

GBAGBA

**WRITTEN By
ROBTEL NEAJAI PAILEY**

Robtel Neajai Pailey

**ILLUSTRATED By
CHASE WALKER**

Gbagba ©2013 by Robtel Neajai Pailey. All rights reserved.

No part of this book may be reproduced, stored in a retrieval system, or transmitted by any means, electronic, mechanical, photocopying, recording, or otherwise, without written permission from the author. For information address One Moore Book, LLC, 751 Franklin Avenue, #116, Brooklyn, NY 11238

Illustrated by Chase Walker
Designed by Steven Melamed

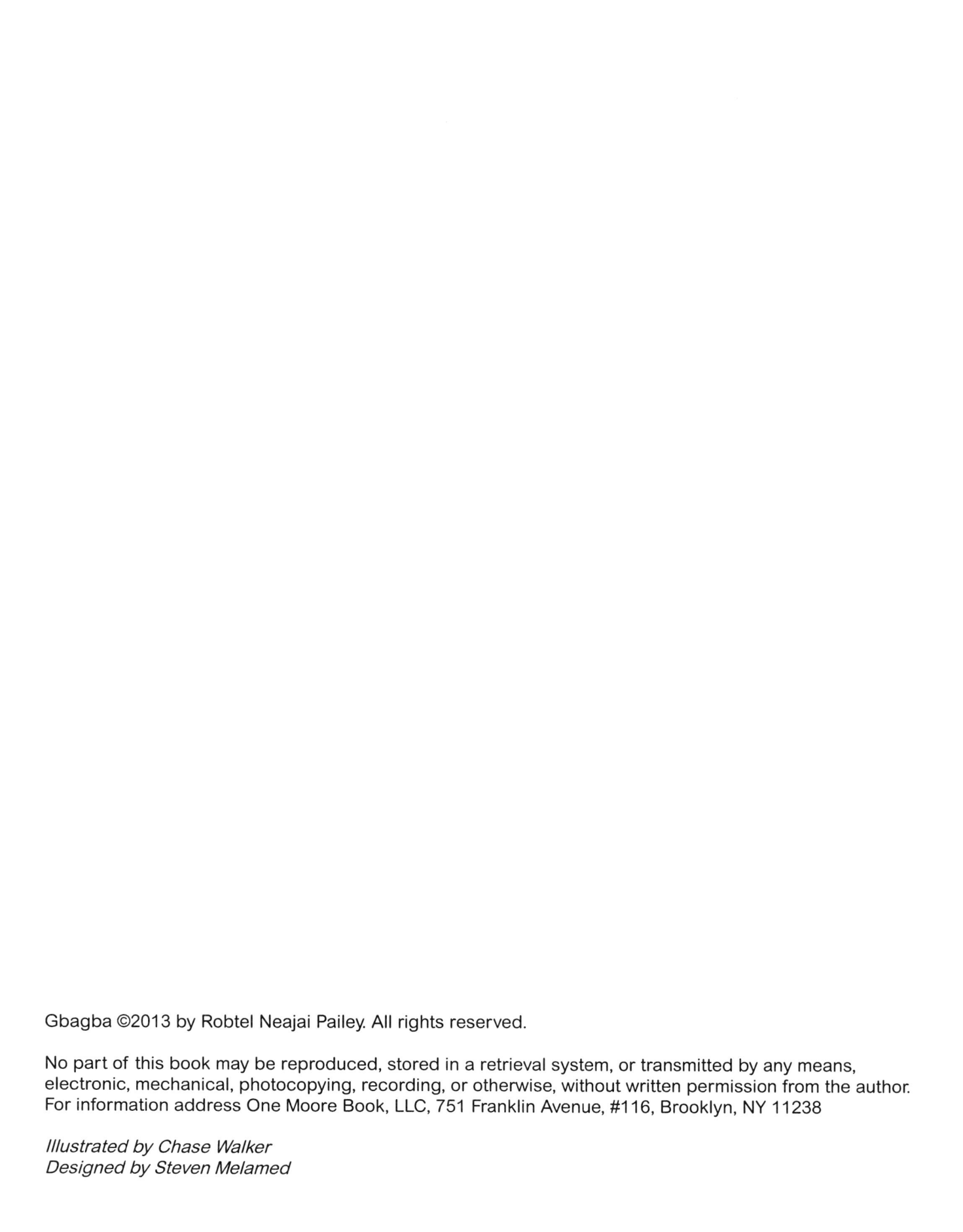

One Moore Book publishes culturally sensitive and educational stories for children of countries with low literacy rates and underrepresented cultures. We provide literature for children whose narratives are largely missing from the children's book publishing industry. The books also serve as a key to unknown people and places for all children who do not have access to cultures outside of their own.

The One Moore Book Store is a distributor of multicultural children's literature from popular and celebrated authors, as well as new and unknown authors whose narratives serve the needs of readers all around the world.

For more information, please visit www.onemoorebook.com

GBAGBA

The Atlantic Ocean made a loud noise outside their bedroom window and Sundaygar and Sundaymah packed their green suitcases with matching handles. The twins moved slowly, as if this would delay their trip. After the last item of clothing was folded neatly into each suitcase, the twins stood together holding hands.

Sundaymah and Sundaygar lived in the port city of Buchanan, the capital of Grand Bassa County in the West African country of Liberia.

"I do not want to go to the capital city, Monrovia. I would rather stay here in Buchanan with Ma and Pa," Sundaymah said to her twin, Sundaygar.

"Come now, Sundaymah," Sundaygar said. "It might be fun to visit Uncle Momo and Auntie Mardie again. Besides, they always spoil us, and it is nice to watch TV whenever we want and to take baths with hot water every day."

Sundaymah's mind went to her busy life in Buchanan. She would miss kicking the football around with Sundaygar in the field near their house.

She would miss eating dumb-boy and hot pepper soup with her bare hands as she sat on the front-porch of Mr. Barchue's store every Saturday afternoon. She would miss walking to school with her best friend Janjay. She would even miss math study class with Ms. Findley, even though fractions were always hard for her to understand.

Most of all, she would miss her Ma and Pa. "Remember that you must behave yourself at Uncle Momo's and Auntie Mardie's," the twins' Ma said. "They have agreed to take you in for two weeks and we do not want you to give them any trouble." The twins nodded. Their Ma knew that her children were just as well behaved as the children in Monrovia, if not more.

When they arrived in Monrovia, Sundaygar and Sundaymah moved their suitcases from the trunk of the taxi. They looked at the many tables with colorful palm nuts, the women who held folded clothes on their heads and the men who pulled wheelbarrows with large jugs of water.

"Sundaymah and Sundaygar!!!" screamed a familiar voice. "Auntie Mardie!!!," they yelled back as they dropped their bags and ran to the woman who looked just like their mother. Auntie Mardie was nicely dressed in a African print dress with her small round glasses sitting on the tip of her nose.

Auntie Mardie asked the driver, Opah, to grab the twins' suitcases. They ran to the black jeep with a red license plate marked RL 507 in slim black letters and numbers. They looked at the license plate and remembered that Auntie Mardie was a big woman in the government. The people in Monrovia called her 'minister.' The twins entered the back door and Auntie Mardie entered the front.

Suddenly, they heard a loud noise coming from the side of the car. People began to scream, "Rogue, rogue, rogue!!!" Sundaymah and Sundaygar looked out of the window as Opah ran behind a man in dirty clothes who had their matching green suitcases in his arms.

The angry crowd made a circle around the rogue like they wanted to harm him. Opah was faster. First he screamed at the man and then he let him go. He grabbed their suitcases and walked to the car. Sundaymah and Sundaygar were relieved.

Opah entered the traffic that led to central Monrovia.

The radio had a special announcement from the president. Her voice stopped the Hip-Co music that came from the speakers. The president usually had a soft voice, but that day her voice sounded as hard as a stone. "Corruption is the enemy," she said. "It is not just in the government that we find this problem. It is everywhere and we must fight it."

Sundaygar and Sundaymah liked the sound of the round "c" word, but they did not know what it meant: *corruption*. They reminded each other that they would have to look it up in Uncle Momo's thick red dictionary, with words so small they had to pinch their eyes to see.

When Opah drove to Vamoma House and Tubman Boulevard, Sundaymah and Sundaygar stared in surprise. The long traffic lines of red, blue, brown and white cars went as far as the eye could see. Like a chorus, the drivers began to honk together loudly. "Don't worry," Auntie Mardie said. "We will find a way out of this traffic."

When the traffic finally moved forward, Opah drove right to the police officer at the junction. "I'm very thirsty," the police officer said standing between the cars. "I want some *cold water* today in this heat." Opah rolled down the window slowly and held out his hand. Sundaymah and Sundaygar both noticed the clean 100 Liberian dollar bill, which the police officer put in his pocket quickly. He waved Opah's car through the traffic in a lane that was not there before.

Sundaymah and Sundaygar were confused by what Opah did and disappointed in the policeman's unfairness to the other drivers. In Buchanan, Ma and Pa always reminded them that they should not jump in front of others in line.

They looked out of the window as they passed the traffic. "Please stop here, Opah. We are going to pick up some snacks for the twins," Auntie Mardie said. Opah drove into the parking lot of a large supermart shaped like a palaver hut, with windows all around.

The twins ran to the sweets section, where they picked up their favorite chocolate bars. When they joined Auntie Mardie in the line, she had a shopping basket with sandwiches, crackers, cheese, biscuits and juice. The twins quietly placed their chocolate bars into the basket of groceries. "So I see you've found some snacks of your own," Auntie Mardie said. She winked at Sundaymah and Sundaygar.

Outside the supermart, Auntie Mardie went to the three women who were selling bananas, paw-paws, and big juicy red, yellow, and green mangoes. As their aunt talked to the fruit sellers, the twins opened their chocolate bars. They looked at each other and spit out the first bite. The bars did not taste like the chocolate they bought in Buchanan. The chocolate they tasted was hard and stale.

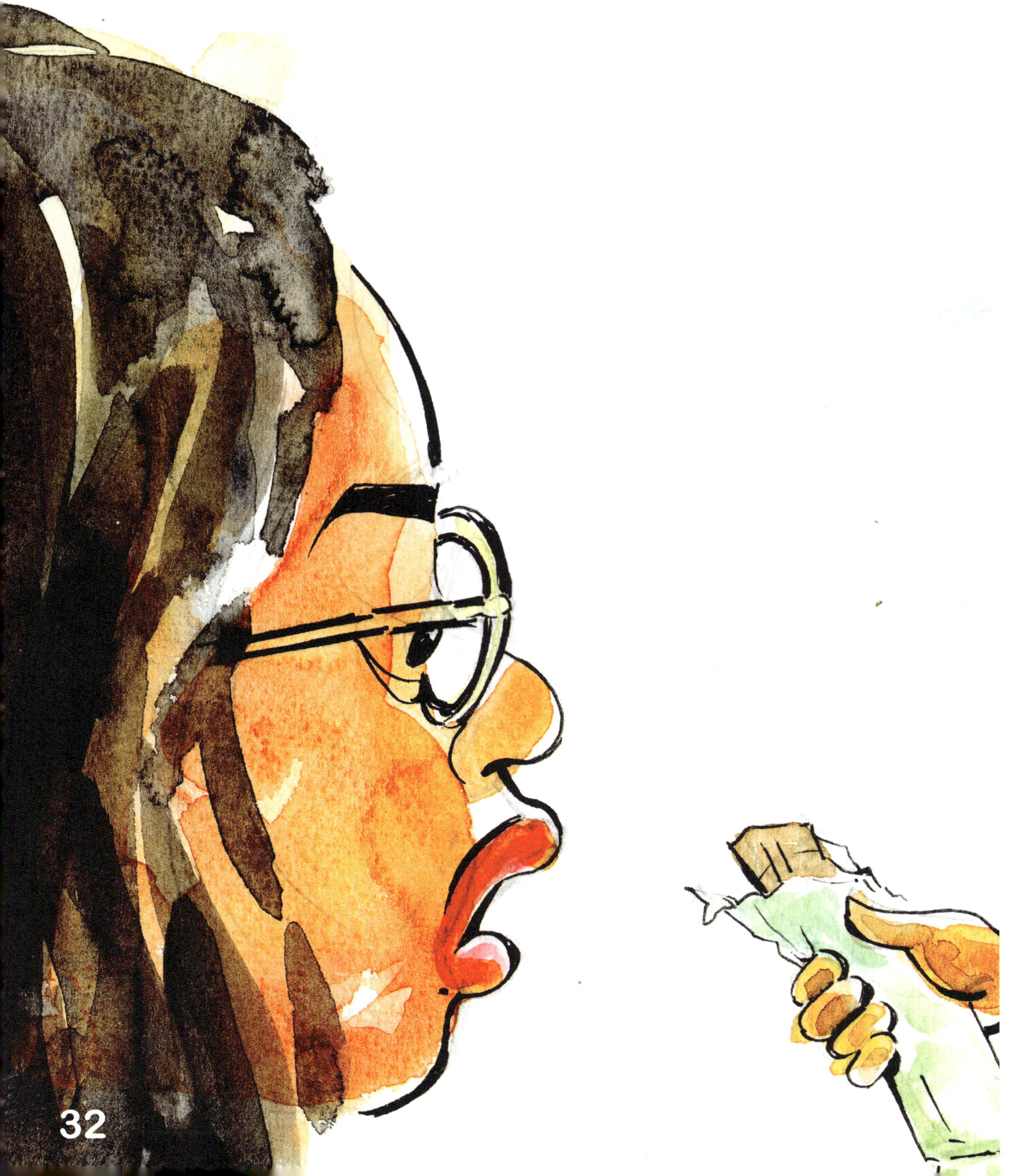

"Auntie Mardie, this chocolate does not taste very good at all," Sundaygar said. Auntie Mardie took the chocolate bars and looked at the expiration dates. "I will be right back," she said to Sundaymah and Sundaygar.

Auntie Mardie went to the store-owner behind the counter. After a minute of talking, she handed the chocolate bars to him and he shook her hand. She smiled at him and left the store.

"What did he say when you told him about the bad-tasting chocolate?" Sundaymah asked. "Don't worry about it, sweetie," Auntie Mardie said.

"Mohammed is a friend of mine, and I have checked his store before for the government. He does not usually have problems with his goods, so I let it go for today."

"But what if he does it again to another person who comes to the store?" Sundaymah and Sundaygar asked.

Auntie Mardie walked away as if she did not hear the twins. They followed her back to the car, shoulders down, and wondered why Auntie Mardie allowed the store-owner to get away with selling bad chocolate.

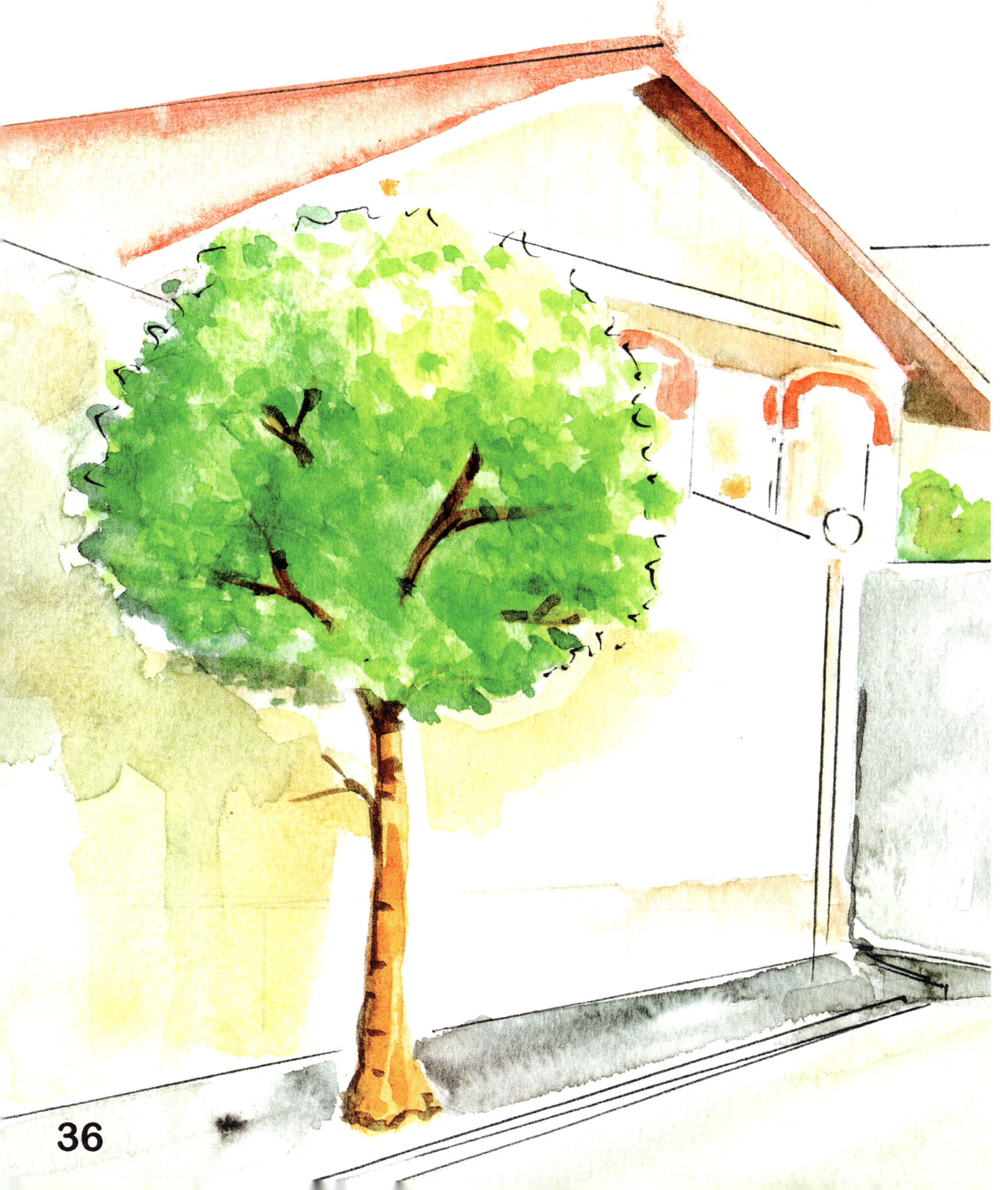

They arrived at their aunt's large house on the Old Road in the suburbs of Monrovia and greeted Uncle Momo, who gave them a bear hug at the door.

After the hug, the twins ran into his office and opened the large dictionary to the word CORRUPTION. They read it out loud together: "Lying, cheating, stealing." They remembered the rogue in the market, the 100 Liberian dollars given to the police officer and the expired chocolate at the grocery store.

Sundaygar and Sundaymah looked at each other and both said the Bassa word *gbagba* [pronounced BAG-BAH], which their parents used to describe lying, cheating, and stealing. *Gbagba* meant trickery, the same as corruption.

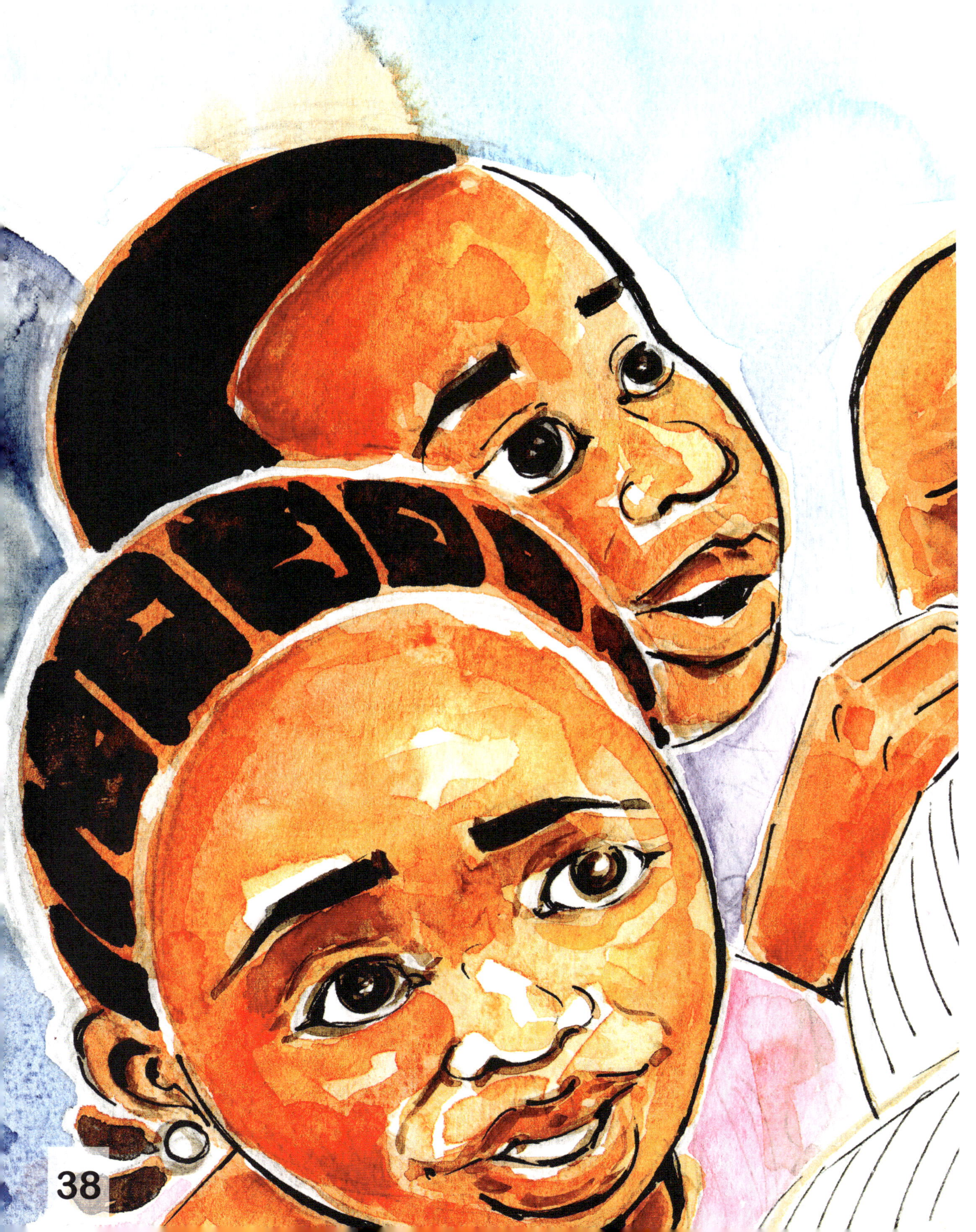

Sundaygar's and Sundaymah's thoughts went to the faces of their parents.

They thought about how Ma and Pa were angry at Mr. Gbezhongar for taking money from their class even though his work was paid by the school. Mr. Gbezhongar had to pay all the families of the students back for the money he took. The principal also moved him from the school.

They thought about how Ma and Pa told the market owners about a woman who sold them rotten pineapples. The market woman said they had to pay for the fruit before they could feel its sharp, spiky skin for holes. After she was reported, the woman had to leave the market.

They thought about how Ma and Pa left their first church, the Pentecostal Tabernacle, because the pastor was caught taking money from the offering to build his family a mansion on the beach.

They thought about *gbagba*, and the round 'c' word. They realized how much they did not like the word at all.

The End

VISIT WWW.ONEMOOREBOOK.COM FOR OUR OTHER TITLES

THE LIBERIA SERIES

J is for Jollof Rice
Story by Wayétu Moore
Illustrated by Kula Moore

1 Peking
Story by Wayétu Moore
Illustrated by Augustus Moore Jr.

My Little Musu
Story by Wiande Moore-Everett and Wayétu Moore
Illustrated by Kula Moore

Kukujumuku
Story by Wayétu Moore
Illustrated by Augustus Moore Jr.

A Gift for Yole
Story by Wayétu Moore
Illustrated by Augustus Moore Jr.

I Love Liberia
Written by Wayétu Moore
Illustrated by Kula Moore

Jamonghoie
Story by Jassie Senwah-Freeman
Written by Wiande Moore-Everett & Wayétu Moore
Illustrated by Augustus Moore Jr.

THE LIBERIA SIGNATURE SERIES

Gbagba
Written by Robtel Pailey
Illustrated by Chase Walker

In Monrovia, When the River Visits the Sea
Written by Patricia Jabbeh Wesley
Illustrated by Kula Moore

What Happened to Red Rooster When a Visitor Came
Written by Stephanie Horton
Illustrated by Chase Walker

THE HAITI SERIES

The Last Mapou (Also in Kreyol)
Written by Edwidge Danticat
Illustrated by Eduoard Duval-Carrie

Elsie
Written by Cybille St. Aude
Illustrated by Marie Cecile Charlier

A is for Ayiti (Also in Kreyol)
Written by Ibi Zoboi
Illustrated by Joseph Zoboi

Fabiola Konn Konte {Fabiola Can Count}
Written by Katia D.Ulysse
Illustrated by Kula Moore

Where is Lola?
Written by Maureen Boyer
Illustrated by Kula Moore

I am riding
Written by M J Fievre
Illustrated by Jean-Patrick Icart

Made in the USA
Charleston, SC
22 March 2014